ROMANCE OF THE THREE KINGDOMS

三國演義

ASIAPAC COMIC SERIES

ROMANCE OF THE THREE KINGDOMS

The Lone Horseman's March
Illustrated by Li Chengli
Adapted by Zhang Qirong
Translated by Yin Shuxun
An Asiapac Publication

② 三國演義

ASIAPAC • SINGAPORE

Publisher
ASIAPAC BOOKS PTE LTD
996 Bendemeer Road #06-08/09
Singapore 339944
Tel: (65) 6392 8455
Fax: (65) 6392 6455
Email: asiapacbooks@pacific.net.sg

Visit us at our Internet home page
www.asiapacbooks.com

Published with the permission of 8 Dragons Publishing & Cultural
Services Ltd, Hong Kong

First published March 1995
2nd edition November 1995
3rd edition January 1999
4th edition June 2002

©1995 ASIAPAC BOOKS, SINGAPORE
ISBN 981-3029-63-3

Cover design by Bay Song Lin
Typeset by Unistar Graphics Pte Ltd
Body text in 8/9 pt Helvetica
Printed in Singapore by
Chung Printing

Publisher's Note

Asiapac Books is proud to bring you a new pictorial series of the famous Chinese novel *Romance of the Three Kingdoms*. Against the backdrop of the tumultuous Three Kingdoms Period, famous battles of Guandu, Yiling and Chibi are brought to life through the skilful hand of Li Chengli.

This second volume is a continuation of the wars, political intrigue and military strategies deployed in the power struggles between the different factions. Find out how legendary heroes like Lu Bu finally met his doom and how Zhang Fei made tragic mistakes because of his drunken state. At the same time, see how the loyal and courageous Guan Yu fought his way through to be reunited with his sworn brothers Liu Bei and Zhang Fei.

We feel honoured to have the permission of 8 Dragons Publishing & Cultural Services to produce this series. We would also like to thank Yin Shuxun for translating this volume and the production team for putting in their best effort in the publication of this book.

Romance of the Three Kingdoms
Vol 1: The Oath of Fraternity in the Peach Garden
Vol 2: The Lone Horseman's March
Vol 3: Zhuge Liang Comes Out of Seclusion
Vol 4: The Battle at the Red Cliff
Vol 5: Zhuge Liang Infuriates Zhou Yu Three Times
Vol 6: Liubei Seizes Xichuan
Vol 7: Guan Yu's Defeat at Maicheng
Vol 8: The Empty-City Ruse
Vol 9: Autumn Wind Blows Across Wuzhangyuan
Vol 10: The Three Kingdoms Merge into Jin

About the Translator

Yin Shuxun 殷书训 (1923 - 1998) was a graduate of the College of Law in Yenching University. He began his career as an editor in the 1950s. He was the editor of *Chinese Literature* and chief editor of Chinese Literature Press, Beijing in the 1980s before retiring in 1991. Being effectively bilingual, he had edited many translated literary works. He was a member of both the All China Writers' Association and All China Translators' Association.

Introduction

Romance of the Three Kingdoms is a graphic presentation of one of China's greatest classical novels. It was written by Luo Guanzhong of the Ming Dynasty who fashioned it into a compelling semi-fictional literary masterpiece.

The novel is based on the history of the period that began towards the end of the Han Dynasty, when three smaller states: Wei, Shu and Wu, were founded and contended for supremacy until the unification of the country by the Jin Dynasty in AD 280. This was a period of great confusion covering nearly a century of complex struggle for power.

You'll read all about the great battles including the battle of Guandu, the battle of the Red Cliff (Chibi), and the battle of Yiling with hundreds of generals, officials and strategists contending one another over political ideas, diplomacy, strategies and military prowess. The novel vividly depicts how different ideas and strategies are debated; how diplomacy is conducted; and how the battles are planned and fought. Some of the philosophies, views and ideas are valued by the Chinese even to this day.

Influenced by the feudalistic culture at that time, the novel has a tendency to glorify Liu Bei, a distant relative of the Han emperor, who later became the king of Shu, while condemning Cao Cao, a formative figure in Chinese history, who usurped the throne of the last emperor of Han and became the king of Wei.

Nevertheless, the more than four hundred historical characters are vividly described in the novel with distinctive individuality and epic grandeur. Among them are familiar historical figures such as the wise and resourceful Zhuge Liang; the kind-hearted and generous Liu Bei; the proud Guan Yu who was a paragon of loyalty; the bold and frank Zhang Fei; the courageous and dauntless Zhao Yun; and the crafty and suspicious Cao Cao.The recurrent themes of power, loyalty and social obligations are important evergreen topics often talked about among the Chinese.

Yin Shuxun

Contents

Guan Yu
(Yunchang)

Liu Bei
(Xuande)

Cao Cao

Yuan Shao

Yan Liang

Tao Qian

Sun Ce

Liu Bei Saves Xuzhou

Soon Li Jue and Guo Si, Dong Zhuo's generals, invaded Chang'an.

They defeated Lü Bu, killed Wang Yun and usurped the throne.

My lords, the Yellow Scarves have risen again!

What shall we do?

All right.

Cao Cao's[1] forces are very strong. Send him to put down the rebels.

Zhu Jun was a court official.

6

1. The Governor of Dongjun.

Cao Cao launched an expedition
and defeated the Yellow Scarves.

Cao Cao reorganised the
surrendered troops and
formed an elite force
called
"Qingzhou Army."

Strategists like Xun Yu, Xun
You, Cheng Yu and Guo Jia all
came to work under Cao Cao.

We would like to
work for you.

Cao Cao recruited many wise and
capable men and expanded his forces.

7

Cao Cao's father, Cao Song was killed by Zhang Kai, Tao Qian's[2] soldier.

Tao Qian allowed his subordinate to kill my father. I won't let him off!

Tao Qian's army was no match for Cao Cao, so he closed the city gates and avoided confrontation.

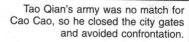

Cao Cao attacked Xuzhou. All the soldiers were dressed in white with a banner, "Revenge" written on it.

Xuzhou is in danger, what should we do?

Let us seek help from Kong Rong[3], and Tien Kai[4]. When their troops arrive, Cao Cao will withdraw.

8

2. Imperial Inspector of Xuzhou.
3. Governor of Beihai.
4. Governor of Qingzhou.

The next day, Liu Bei borrowed 2,000 soldiers from Gongsun Zan. Together with General Zhao Yun and his own men, they set off for Xuzhou.

When Liu Bei arrived in Xuzhou, he joined forces with those led by Kong Rong and Tien Kai.

All right.

Guan Yu and Zhao Yun will assist you. Zhang Fei and I will fight Cao Cao, then enter the city to join Governor Tao.

Liu Bei and Zhang Fei led their troops and charged into Cao Cao's encampment.

Yu Jin, one of Cao Cao's generals fought back.

Zhang Fei defeated Yu Jin.

Tao Qian opened the gate to receive Liu Bei and Zhang Fei.

Liu Bei is a hero. I am old and feeble. Let's ask him to take over Xuzhou.

Tao Qian held a banquet.

Mi Zhu, get me the official seal of Xuzhou.

Yes, my lord.

12

13

Cao Cao withdrew his troops.

Tao Qian was very happy Cao Cao withdrew his troops. He held a feast in the city.

You're virtuous and talented. Please accept this seal of Xuzhou.

I saved Xizhou to uphold justice. I'll be condemned if I take over Xuzhou.

General Liu, Governor Tao is sincere. Accept this offer and accomplish meritorious deeds.

No, I cannot accept.

Governor Tao is old and sick. Please accept the offer.

15

17

Kong Rong and
Tien Kai then left.

Liu Bei bade Zhao Yun a
tearful farewell.

Goodbye,
Zilong.

Liu Bei went to Xiaopei with
Guan Yu and Zhang Fei to reassure
the people that everything was fine.

18

The Fierce Battle at Puyang

Cao Cao withdrew his troops and met Cao Ren on his way back.

We are no match for Lü Bu. We've lost both Yanzhou and Puyang.

Lü Bu is brave but has no strategy. We need not fear him.

Xue Lan and Li Feng, defend Yanzhou with your troops. I'll defend Puyang. We'll support one another in this way.

News of Cao Cao's return reached Yanzhou.

21

My lord, as the mountain path here is perilous, there may be an ambush.

Cao Cao's troops reached Tai Mountain.

Lü Bu has no strategies. His adjutant officers are guarding Yanzhou and his own troops are at Puyang. We won't be ambushed here. March forward.

Cao Cao sent Cao Ren and his men to surround Yanzhou. Then he and his men marched towards Puyang.

The next day, the two armies met on the battlefield.

I have no grudges against you. Why did you seize my cities?

These cities belong to the Han empire. Everyone has a share.

Lü Bu's general, Zang Ba challenged Yue Jin, Cao Cao's general, but neither emerged the winner.

Xiahou Dun went to Yue Jin's aid. Lü Bu's general, Zhang Liao met him head on.

Getting impatient, Lü Bu swung his halberd and charged towards the enemy on a steed called *Red Rabbit*.

Lü Bu was invincible and Cao Cao's forces were driven back.

Lü Bu held a banquet to celebrate his victory.

Xizhai is a strategic war zone. Guard against a sneak attack by Cao Cao.

Cao Cao is a good military tactician. We'd better be on guard.

They've just lost a battle. They won't dare to make a sneak attack.

Lü Bu sent his three generals, Gao Shun, Wei Xu and Hou Cheng to Xizhai.

As expected, Cao Cao launched a sneak attack on Xizhai.

25

As Lü Bu was well prepared, Cao Cao's army was again defeated.

Chen Gong had another stratagem for Lü Bu.

Good stratagem!

Cao Cao was upset after two consecutive defeats.

Just then, he received a secret letter.

"Lü Bu has left. You can attack the city at midnight. I'll be your planted agent."

Heaven is helping me to recapture Puyang.

Cao Cao rewarded the messenger and promptly ordered an attack.

Yes.

Lü Bu is no strategist but Chen Gong is cunning. Be careful.

Liu Ye was Cao Cao's adviser.

Cao Cao and his men arrived in Puyang at midnight.

Xiahou Dun and Cao Hong, each of you lead a contingent outside the city.

Yes.

My lord, you mustn't risk your life.

Xiahou Yuan, Li Dian, Yue Jin and Dian Wei, we'll attack the city.

I must. If I don't, who will?

Soon, a signal was heard and the gate swung open.

Charge!

Cao Cao rode into the city.

They charged into the governor's mansion but it was empty.

We're been tricked! Withdraw immediately!

28

Boom!

Boom!

Boom!

"Don't let Cao Cao escape!"

Cao Cao, you can't escape now!

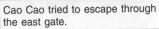

Cao Cao tried to escape through the east gate.

Cao Cao, you can't run away!

He rode towards the gate.

Dian Wei protected Cao Cao and held up the two generals.

In the confusion.
Cao Cao rode to the
north gate.

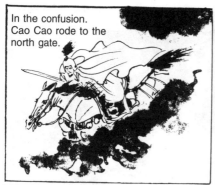

He brushed passed Lü Bu.

On no!
I'll have
to charge
forward.

Lü Bu galloped towards Cao Cao.

Did you see
Cao Cao?

He's on
the brown
horse in
front!

Lü Bu struck Cao Cao on the
helmet with his halberd.

Lü Bu rode on in pursuit.

Cao Cao hurried towards the east gate.

He met Dian Wei.

Follow me, my lord.

A burning beam fell and crushed Cao Cao's horse. Cao Cao was burnt.

Dian Wei and Xiahou Yuan helped Cao Cao to escape.

I fell into their trap. I'll definitely take revenge.

He ordered the army to be dressed in mourning clothes to indicate that he'd died.

Cao Cao reckoned that Lü Bu would launch an attack so he laid an ambush at Maling Hill.

Ha! Ha! Cao Cao's dead. I'll annihilate his army.

Ah! Cao Cao! I've been fooled.

Charge! Kill them!

Lü Bu was severely defeated and fled back to Puyang.

When a plague hit Puyang, Cao Cao and Lü Bu ceased fighting. Cao Cao then moved to Juancheng.

Meanwhile, Tao Qian died and Liu Bei was put in charge of Xuzhou.

Liu Bei took Xuzhou without effort. It makes me mad! I'll seize it from him.

My lord, if you attack Xuzhou before seizing Yanzhou, you're neglecting the important. What if Lü Bu attacks us?

The Yellow Scarves have stored grain in Runan and Yingchuan...

What's your view?

Cao Cao accepted Xun Yu's suggestion. He attacked and seized Runan and Yingchuan.

He also recruited a fierce warrior, Xu Chu.

With his well-trained troops and sufficient grain supply, Cao Cao recaptured Yanzhou.

Then he appointed Dian Wei and Xu Chu as the vanguard of the army to attack Puyang.

My lord, Cao Cao's army is here.

Gao Shun and Zhang Liao are supervising grain transportation. We'll fight only when they're back.

Lü Bu refused to listen to Chen Gong's advice and was defeated by Cao Cao.

A rich man of Puyang named Tien surrendered the city to Cao Cao. Lü Bu escaped to Dingtao.

Cao Cao led the victorious army in pursuit and defeated Lü Bu again.

After his defeat, Lü Bu went to Liu Bei and sought shelter at Xuzhou.

From then on, Cao Cao had control of Shandong.

Soon afterwards, Li Jue and Guo Si had a power struggle in court.

Han Xiandi issued an edict to Cao Cao, asking for his protection.

Li Jue and Guo Si were defeated and fled to Xiliang.

Cao Cao coerced the emperor to move the capital to Xudu.

Cao Cao usurped power and became an overlord of the dukes and princes.

The Drunken Zhang Fei Loses Xuzhou

Now that Lü Bu had joined Liu Bei, Cao Cao was worried that they would attack Xudu. He summoned his advisors to the court.

Xun Yu suggested using a stratagem, "Make two tigers fight over food".

Send an emissary to confer on Liu Bei the title, Governor of Xuzhou and give him a secret letter, asking him to kill Lü Bu.

A good idea!

Cao Cao sent an emissary to bring the edict and a secret letter to Liu Bei.

Liu Bei had a discussion with Guan Yu and Zhang Fei.

Lü Bu is a treacherous person. Let's kill him!

Lü Bu has sought help from me. It's not humane to kill him.

41

Rest be assured. I won't fall into his trap.

Thank you. I will leave how.

Cao Cao wants to gain at our expense. We shouldn't be fooled by him.

Why don't you get rid of Lü Bu?

I'll kill Lü Bu no matter what Cao Cao's plot is.

You're right.

We'll use another stratagem, "Drive the tiger to swallow the wolf".

Cao Cao again consulted Xun Yu.

The emissary went back and told Cao Cao that Liu Bei wouldn't kill Lü Bu as ordered.

43

44

Liu Bei then led an expedition against Yuan Shu.

Zhang Fei now only managed military affairs and Chen Deng managed the day-to-day affairs.

I've stopped drinking for too long. I want to drink now!

Zhang Fei held a big feast.

Today we can drink to our fill. We'll stop drinking from tomorrow onwards.

Zhang Fei proposed a drink to everyone. He went up to Cao Bao.

How can a man not drink?

Sorry, I don't drink.

45

Cao Bao was forced to drink a cup of wine.

Zhang Fei drank too much and got drunk.

Here, have another drink!

I can't drink any more, General Zhang.

Cao Bao refused.

How dare you! Guards, gives him a hundred lashes.

You're a civil officer. It's none of your business!

Chen Deng tried to dissuade Zhang Fei.

46

47

Eldest Brother, we've lost Xuzhou.

She's trapped in Xuzhou.

Where's eldest sister-in-law?

Liu Bei was in battle with Yuan Shu at Xuyi.

What did you say before? Now you've lost the city and eldest sister-in-law is trapped there...

We have pledged to die together. What's the big deal about losing the city and family? Why must you kill yourself?

Zhang Fei attempted to kill himself.

Eldest brother, I've let you down!

48

Learning that Lü Bu had captured Xuzhou, Yuan Shu promised Lü Bu a handsome gift if he'd agree to attack Liu Bei.

Lü Bu sent Gao Shun to lead 50,000 troops to attack Liu Bei.

Go back and tell Lü Bu that I'll send the gift once Liu Bei is killed.

Liu Bei hurriedly withdrew his troops from Xuyi and attacked Guangling.

When Gao Shun reached Xuyi, he asked Yuan Shu for the gift that Lü Bu had been promised.

Yuan Shu has broken his promise. I'll fight him!

Yuan Shu is powerful. We'd better give Xiaopei back to Liu Bei and join forces with him to fight Yuan Shu.

Good, we'll do that.

Defeated at Guangling, Liu Bei was glad to go back to Xuzhou.

Lü Bu sent Liu Bei's family members back. Liu Bei then went to Xiaopei to station his troops.

Sun Ce, the Young Conqueror

After Sun Jian's death, his son, Sun Ce, returned to the Yangtze River with his remaining troops. His family moved to Qu'e where his uncle, Wu Jing, was the Governor of Danyang.

Sun Ce's forces were weak so he had to serve under Yuan Shu and was made the Commander of Righteousness.

Yuan Shu sent Sun Ce to lead several expeditions and he won many battles.

Oh! I would die without regret if I had a son like Sun Ce.

Sigh....

Once, angered by Yuan Shu, Sun Ce returned to his camp.

Why are you sighing?

Zhu Zhi was Sun Jian's former subordinate.

My father was a brave soldier yet I've to seek shelter under others…

Liu You[1] has seized Qu'e. Ask Lord Yuan for troops to rescue Qu'e and prepare to fulfil your ambition.

I can lend you 100 of my elite soldiers.

Lü Fan, an advisor of Yuan Shu, entered Sun Ce's camp.

1. *Provincial Governor of Yangzhou.*

53

I'll use the imperial seal left by my father as a pledge.

Yuan Shu won't lend you his troops.

Thus, Sun Ce was able to borrow 3,000 troops from Yuan Shu.

Together with Zhu Zhi, Lü Fan, Cheng Pu, Huang Gai and Han Dang, Sun Ce went to Qu'e with his troops.

I'd like to work under you.

Passing through Liyang, Sun Ce met Zhou Yu, his sworn brother.

Zhou Yu recommended Zhang Zhao and Zhang Hong to be Sun Ce's advisors.

Sun Ce defeated Zhang Ying, Liu You's general at Niuzhu and captured 4,000 soldiers.

Jiang Qin and Zhou Tai led 300 men to join Sun Ce's army.

One day, Sun Ce and his generals surveyed Liu You's encampment.

Sun Ce's army advanced to Shentingling. Liu You and his troops encamped in the south.

55

My lord, Sun Ce is surveying our encampment.

This must be a ruse.

If we don't capture Sun Ce now, when will we? Follow me.

Taishi Ci is a brave warrior; I'll help him.

I am Sun Ce. Who are you?

Who is Sun Ce?

Taishi Ci charged up the hill.

I'm Taishi Ci of Donglai, here to capture you.

Taishi Ci charged towards Sun Ce.

They fought for 50 rounds but neither won.

Feigning defeat, Taishi Ci fled and then returned to fight with Sun Ce again.

They fought with their bare hands.

Each got hold of the other's spear, struggled and fell from their horses.

When Liu You came to Taishi Ci's aid, Cheng Pu also came to Sun Ce's aid.

Sun Ce only had a small force. Zhou Yu came with his troops and joined the battle. Finally both sides withdrew to their own camps.

I'll launch a sneak attack on Qu'e. Liu You will surely be defeated.

Good!

Sun Ce returned to his camp.

Zhou Yu attacked and captured Qu'e that night.

When Liu You learned about this, he withdrew his troops.

Sun Ce routed Liu You's troops.

Sun Ce then led his army to attack Moling. But Xue Li, the Garrison Commander, decided to defend the city.

Taishi Ci had to flee to Jingxian.

Liu You is going to seize Niuzhu.

Yu Mi, Liu You's general, was captured by Sun Ce in only three rounds.

Sun Ce led his forces to Niuzhu to confront Liu You.

Fan Neng came to Yu Mi's rescue.

Fan Neng fell from his horse and died.

Sun Ce crushed Yu Mi to death.

He's really a young conqueror!

A defeated Liu You joined Liu Biao.

After seizing Moling, Sun Ce and Zhou Yu proceeded to capture Taishi Ci.

Zhou Yu tied up Taishi Ci. Sun Ce came and untied him.

I will gather Liu You's remaining soldiers and serve you. Can you trust me?

Good! I'll expect all of you tomorrow at noon.

He will. He's trustworthy.

He won't be back.

The next day, Taishi Ci came back with the soldiers.

General Sun!

Sun Ce then captured Wujun, Kuaiji and other cities. Soon, he occupied the whole area south of the Yangtze River.

The Death of Lü Bu

Soon, Yuan Shu sent General Ji Ling to attack Liu Bei.

Liu Bei sent an envoy to ask Lü Bu for help.

I'll set my halberd at the gate. If I hit it, you must call off the fight.

Lü Bu's arrow hit the target so the fight was called off.

Lü Bu pressed them to call off the fight.

A few days later, Lü Bu attacked Xiaopei because Zhang Fei seized some of his horses.

Cao Cao appointed Liu Bei as Perfect of Yuzhou.

Cao Cao was about to attack Lü Bu.

Zhang Xiu of Wancheng has declared that he'll attack the capital and kidnap the emperor.

Appoint Lü Bu as Governor of Xuzhou. Get him to make peace with Liu Bei.

I'll suppress Zhang Xiu, but what if Lü Bu attacks Xudu?

Cao Cao attacked Wenchang and Zhang Xiu surrendered.

Cao Cao took Lady Zou as his concubine.

Enraged, Zhang Xiu raided Cao Cao's camp in the night and killed the warrior Dian Wei. Cao Cao had to flee back to Xudu.

Before long, Yuan Shu proclaimed himself emperor of Shouchun. Cao Cao attacked Shouchun with the help of Lü Bu and Sun Ce.

Cao Cao ordered Liu Bei to station his troops in Xiaopei to guard against Lü Bu.

He then mobilised his troops again to fight Zhang Xiu but was again defeated by him and Liu Biao of Jingzhou.

67

Cao Cao wrote to Liu Bei, asking him to join forces to attack Lü Bu. But Lü Bu attacked Xiaopei first.

Liu Bei was defeated and Xiaopei fell.

Cao Cao defeated Lü Bu time and again; and occupied Xuzhou and Xiaopei.

Encamp outside the city – I'll guard it with the remaining forces. When Cao Cao's supply is exhausted, we can defeat him.

A good idea!

Lü Bu had retreated to Xiapi.

I'll station some troops outside the city.

Where are you going?

Lü Bu went home to pack up.

68

69

Tear down the embankment of the Yihe and Sishui to flood the city.

Cao Cao adopted Guo Jia's stratagem and flooded the area.

The city is flooded!

I've my *Red Rabbit* steed. What's there to be afraid of?

He drank even more to smother his anxiety.

Lü Bu looked into the mirror.

I look so pale! It must be the drinking. I'll quit drinking from today.

Issue an order. From today, drinking is prohibited. Whoever disobeys will be executed!

Just then, General Hou Cheng came back with fifteen stolen horses.

What'll we do if Lü Bu finds out?

I'll present him with some excellent wine.

Hou Cheng wanted to celebrate by drinking.

My men have come to celebrate with me. Have some wine, my lord.

I've just prohibited drinking. Are you rebelling against me? Execute him!

Song Xian and Wei Xu carried Hou Cheng home.

If it hadn't been for you, I would have died.

Lü Bu is ruthless. Let's surrender the city to Cao Cao.

Good!

Hou Cheng stole Lü Bu's horse, *Red Rabbit*, went to Cao Cao's camp and surrendered.

73

With help from conspirators in the city, Xiapi finally fell.

Lü Bu, Chen Gong, Gao Shun and Zhang Liao were captured.

Cao Cao also wanted to execute Zhang Liao.

He's an honourable man, I'll vouch for him with my life.

Cao Cao left Cavalry Commander Che Zhou to guard Xuzhou. Then he left for Xudu with Liu Bei.

Zhang Liao surrendered to Cao Cao. Cao Cao appointed him as Garrison Commander.

Cao Cao Warms the Wine and Comments on Distinguished Heroes

Cao Cao returned to Xudu. Liu Bei stayed in a house near his residence.

It would be harmful to have Liu Bei as an imperial uncle.

As an emperor, I can order him around, what's there to fear?

He brought Liu Bei to see Xiandi. Liu Bei was found to be a distant uncle so Xiandi appointed him as a Senior General.

Not long after, Cao Cao usurped power of the court so the emperor wrote a secret decree with his own blood to kill Cao Cao.

He gave the secret decree to the royal brother-in-law, Dong Cheng.

Dong Cheng allied with Wang Zifu and Ma Teng, and pledged to kill Cao Cao.

I will join the alliance!

Liu Bei signed the pact.

Dong Zheng asked Liu Bei to join them.

Afraid of arousing Cao Cao's suspicion, Liu Bei grew vegetables in his backyard everyday.

Why are you growing vegetables instead of attending to state affairs?

I have my reasons.

One day Xu Chu and Zhang Liao came to the vegetable garden.

Imperial Uncle Liu, the Prime Minister wants to see you immediately.

Don't tell me...

Liu Bei was secretly alarmed.

We don't know.

Anything urgent?

What important work are you doing at home?

Liu Bei went to the Prime Minister's residence, feeling uneasy.

Come with me to my back garden.

Liu Bei went pale with fright.

Who knows what he's up to? I've to be careful.

Your vegetation is doing well!

Oh, it's just to pass time.

Liu Bei was relieved.

Look at the plums! Let's have some wine.

The plums remind me of an incident during my expedition against Zhang Xiu.

The soldiers were thirsty.

There's a plum forest ahead. Let's go!

The soldiers were not thirsty anymore.

While they were drinking, the sky darkened.

Let me test his courage.

Who do you think can be considered the most illustrious man of our time?

84

85

And who has these qualities?

Ha! Ha! At the present moment, only you and I!

Liu Bei dropped his chopsticks.

87

Advance quickly!

I won't forget.

Don't forget our alliance!

I was a caged bird in Xudu but now, I've soared into the sky.

What's the hurry?

Tell Cao Cao that I've to ignore his orders.

Dong Cheng came to bid Liu Bei goodbye.

Cao Cao wanted to call Liu Bei back.

89

Liu Bei arrived in Xuzhou and defeated Yuan Shu.

Che Zhou, the Governor of Xuzhou, received Cao Cao's letter, asking him to get rid of Liu Bei.

The secret leaked out. Che Zhou was killed by Guan Yu and Zhang Fei.

Liu Bei recaptured Xuzhou and prepared to oppose Cao Cao.

Yuan Shu died soon after his defeat.

Guan Yu Surrenders to Cao Cao

The next year, Dong Cheng conspired with the court physician, Ji Ping, to poison Cao Cao.

Dong Cheng, Wang Zifu and their families were killed.

The conspiracy was found out. Ji Ping was arrested so he killed himself.

Cao Cao found the royal decree written in blood and the pact of alliance.

Ma Teng and Liu Bei are still at large. I'll not let them off!

I'll suppress Liu Bei. What do you think?

Cao Cao had a discussion with Cheng Yu and Guo Jia.

Liu Bei's soldiers are all new recruits. If you launch an eastern expedition, you'll succeed.

If you don't suppress Liu Bei now, it will be difficult to do so later.

Yuan Shao is stationed in Guandu. What if he attacks us while you're fighting Liu Bei?

Cao Cao set off for Xuzhou with 200,000 men.

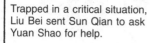

Trapped in a critical situation, Liu Bei sent Sun Qian to ask Yuan Shao for help.

Sun Qian went with Tian Feng to see Yuan Shao.

Since Cao Cao is on his eastern expedition, we should attack Xudu.

My youngest son is ill. I can't launch an expedition.

94

95

As Cao Cao was well prepared, he defeated Liu Bei and Zhang Fei.

Zhang Fei had to flee to the Mangdang hills.

Liu Bei sought Yuan Shao's aid.

Having captured Xuzhou and Xiaopei, Cao Cao asked his advisors about the next move.

Guan Yu is taking care of Liu Bei's family and is now defending Xiapi. Attack him at once.

97

Enraged, Guan Yu led a force of 3,000 men out of the city to fight Cao Cao's men.

Xiahou Dun met him head on.

He feigned defeat and rode away, luring Guan Yu away from Xiapi.

I fell into their trap. I must go back to the city.

Bong!

Xu Huang and Xu Zhu intercepted Guan Yu.

Guan Xu fought very hard but couldn't break through the encirclement. He retreated to a hill.

Cao Cao's informants opened the city gate. Cao Cao charged into Xiapi.

He set fire to the city.

Guan Yu saw the fire in Xiapi.

Xiapi is lost and my two sisters-in-law are trapped. I must fight back.

He charged down the hill.

101

However, he was held back by many arrows.

At daybreak, Cao Cao sent Zhang Liao to see Guan Yu.

You're now in an impasse, what's your plan?

You can kill me but I'll fight till I die.

Firstly, you'll violate the oath made at the Peach Garden to die together with your brothers.

If you die in battle, you'd have committed 3 sins.

What are they?

Secondly, you'll not be able to protect Liu Bei's family as promised.

Thirdly, you should help General Liu Bei to save the Han Dynasty. You can't just die for no reason!

Surrender for now, then join Liu Bei when you know where he is.

What do you want me to do?

I'll do so if Cao Cao agrees to 3 conditions.

I'll tell him.

Firstly, Guan Yu will surrender to the Emperor but not to Prime Minister Cao Cao.

Zhang Liao went back to Cao Cao.

I'm the Prime Minister of the Han Empire. Surrendering to the Han Emperor means surrendering to me. Agreed!

Secondly, his two sisters-in-law must not be violated.

Agreed.

Thirdly, once he knows Liu Bei's whereabouts, he'll join him.

I can't agree to that.

He is loyal to Liu Bei because of his kindness. If you surpass Liu Bei in this respect, he'll stay.

That's true. I agree.

Zhang Liao told Guan Yu that Cao Cao had agreed to his conditions. Guan Yu then surrendered his troops.

Cao Cao returned to Xudu triumphantly the next day.

Guan Yu had the carriages ready for his sisters-in-law and escorted them to Xudu.

Cao Cao gave Guan Yu a house to stay.

Guan Yu let his sisters-in-law stay in the inner court.

Cao Cao presented Guan Yu to Xiandi. The Emperor conferred on him the title of Assistant Commander.

Cao Cao gave Guan Yu beautiful girls and a lot of gold, silver and brocade.

Let them serve my sisters-in-law.

One day Cao Cao presented him with a new brocade robe.

Why do you have to be so frugal, Yunchang?

The old robe was a gift from brother Liu Bei. It reminds me of him.

What a chivalrous man!

Thank you, Your Excellency.

Soon after, Cao Cao gave Guan Yu Lü Bu's horse.

109

The Fierce Battle at
White Horse Slope

When Yuan Shao's son recovered from his illness, Yuan Shao contemplated attacking Cao Cao.

Cao Cao's forces are now very strong. It's not time to attack them.

What's your view, General Liu?

Cao Cao is the usurper. We should launch an expedition against him.

If my lord doesn't listen to me, the expedition will be unsuccessful.

Yuan Shao was angry with Tien Feng for disagreeing with him. He was later put in jail.

Together with Liu Bei, Yuan Shao set off with his expeditionary force.

He appointed General Yan Liang as commander of the vanguard troops for the battle at White Horse Slope.

Cao Cao confronted Yuan's army there.

113

115

Guan Yu came to White Horse Slope the next day.

I sent for you because Yan Liang killed my generals.

Rest be assured, Your Excellency, I'll kill him!

Guan Yu charged into the enemy's camp and headed straight for Yan Liang.

117

Yuan Shao met one of Yan Liang's soldiers.

A red-faced long bearded warrior killed the general!

The emperor bestowed on Guan Yu the title of Han Duke of Shou'ting. A gold seal was specially cast for him.

He must be Guan Yu, Liu Bei's sworn brother.

Who is this man?

Arrest Liu Bei and execute him!

Many people look alike in the world. How can you be sure it was Guan Yu?

That's true.

119

Liu Bei asked to go with Wen Chou. Yuan Shao gave him 30,000 troops to help Wen Chou.

Cao Cao learned that Wen Chou had crossed the Yellow River. He decided to confront him.

I'll lure the enemy into my trap.

What if the enemy grabs our supply?

We'll wait and see.

Place our food supply in front, the combat unit at the back.

Cao Cao's advisor, Lü Qian was not convinced.

Wen Chou's troops soon arrived and seized Cao Cao's food supply.

Let's take a rest. Release the horses.

We've lost our food supply!

The enemy is here, let's retreat.

We should lure the enemy here. Why should we retreat?

121

Cao Cao winked at Xun You and smiled.

Eh....

Attack!

Yuan Shao's troops seized the food supply and horses.

123

Guan Yu and Wen Chou fought for three rounds. Wen Chou was eventually hacked down from his horse by Guan Yu.

Cao Cao seized back all the supplies and won a resounding victory.

125

126

The Lone Horseman's
1,000-*li* March

Liu Bei wants you to join him.

Liu Bei sent a messenger to take a letter to Guan Yu.

I'll bid Cao Cao farewell and leave with my two sisters-in-law.

Since I know my brother's whereabouts, I won't stay here.

What if he refuses to let you go?

Guan Yu wanted to see Cao Cao but Cao Cao avoided him.

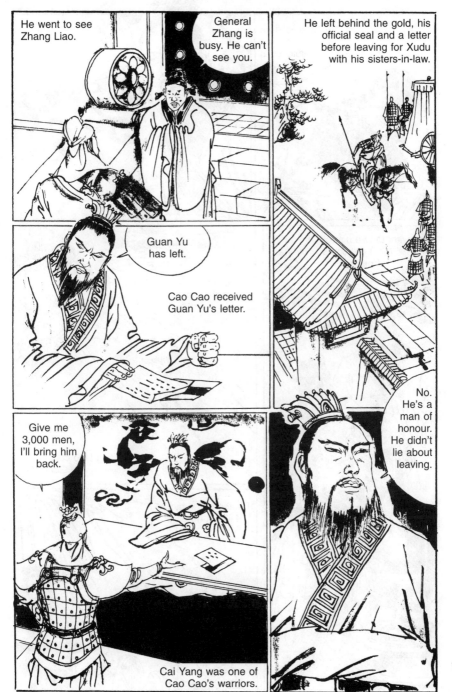

He went to see Zhang Liao.

General Zhang is busy. He can't see you.

He left behind the gold, his official seal and a letter before leaving for Xudu with his sisters-in-law.

Guan Yu has left.

Cao Cao received Guan Yu's letter.

No. He's a man of honour. He didn't lie about leaving.

Give me 3,000 men, I'll bring him back.

Cai Yang was one of Cao Cao's warriors.

129

If he joins Yuan Shao, there'll be trouble. Let's kill him.

I've given him my word. He joined Liu Bei out of loyalty.

I want to see him off. Tell him I will come at once.

Yes.

Yunchang, wait!

Zhang Liao caught up with Guan Yu.

Please go ahead. I'll wait here.

131

Then I'll give you a brocaded robe.

Being cautious, Guan Yu picked up the robe with the tip of his sword.

Thank you, Your Excellency. Goodbye.

He's rude! I'll capture him!

He's right to be suspicious. Let him go.

Guan Yu and his sisters-in-law were warmly received by Hu Hua, the head of a village.

My son works under Wang Zhi.[1] Please give my son this letter.

I will.

Guan Yu and his group arrived at Dongling Pass.

Guan Yu killed Kong Xiu who refused to let him through.

Governor Han Fu of Loyang and Commander Meng Tan held a secret discussion.

I'll engage Guan Yu in battle and you'll fire an arrow at him. We'll take him to Xudu for a reward.

133

1. The Governor of Yingyang.

That's a good idea.

Guan Yu came to Loyang but was blocked by Han Fu.

Do you want to die just like Kong Xiu?

Guan Yu, I've come to fight you!

Guan Yu brought Meng Tan down after only 3 rounds.

Han Fu's arrow hit Guan Yu's left arm.

You scoundrel, look out!

Guan Yu killed Han Fu in one swoop of his sword.

General Bian Xi laid an ambush at Zhenguo Temple.

I had to kill the guards. Please let me through.

I, Bian Xi, welcome General Guan.

I'll escort you out of the Pass.

Bian Xi held a feast for Guan Yu at Zhenguo Temple.

The abbot of the temple invited Guan Yu to his room for tea.

Please take care....

How dare you trap me?

136

Guan Yu killed Bian Xi.

Guan Yu reached Yingyang Pass.

Wang Zhi invited Guan Yu to stay in a hostel.

General Guan, you must pack and leave at once.

Guan Yu left the hostel with his sisters-in-law hurriedly.

Thank you.

Hu Ban got the gatekeeper to open the gate.

When Wang Zhi heard about the escape, he went in pursuit of Guan Yu.

Guan Yu then arrived
at the Yellow River.

Qin Qi, Xiahou Dun's subordinate, refused to let Guan Yu pass through.

Guan Yu charged through the Pass and killed him.

He and his men then crossed the river.

Soon after, Xiahou Dun and his troops caught up with them.

141

142

Let me capture him alive. The Prime Minister can release him later.

Cao Cao gave orders to let him pass.

Zhang Liao arrived.

I was forced to kill those men. Please ask Cao Cao to pardon me.

Guan Yu arrived at Woniu Mountain. He recruited an outlaw, Zhou Cang.

Guan Yu learned that Zhang Fei had seized a fort. He went there and they were reunited.

Soon afterwards, Liu Bei found a chance to escape from Yuan Shao's camp with Jian Yong and Sun Qian.

On his way to Gucheng, Liu Bei met Zhao Yun and they travelled together.

The three sworn brothers were finally reunited.

I'll reorganize my army and gain control of the Central Plain!

Sun Quan Assumes Command of Jiangdong

After conquering the land east of the Yangtze River, Sun Ce captured Lujiang and Yuzhang prefectures.

He sent Zhang Hong to Xudu to report his victorious expeditions.

This little lion is really ferocious and very hard to handle.

Cao Cao bethrothed Cao Ren's daughter to Sun Kuang, Sun Ce's younger brother.

No, that's impossible.

General Sun asks you to appoint him as Chief Commanding Officer.

Zhang Hong, stay in Xudu.

Eh....

I'll fight my way to Xudu. Let's see whether Cao Cao dares to look down on me.

I'll report this to the Prime Minister.

Xu Gong, the Governor of Wujun, came to hear about Sun Ce.

Zhang Hong sent a messenger to tell Sun Ce about Cao Cao's attitude.

That rat, I'll kill him!

The messenger was caught and Sun Ce read the letter.

He wrote a secret letter to be sent to Xudu.

Invite Xu Gong to come here. Tell him I've important matters to discuss with him.

Xu Gong came to see Sun Ce and was hanged.

We must avenge our master!

Xu Gong's subordinates were angry.

One day, Sun Ce went hunting with Cheng Pu at the Western Hills.

Xu Gong's subordinates followed them secretly.

Look, a big deer! Give chase!

148

149

Sun Ce pulled out the arrow and shot it back with his bow.

Sun Ce was wounded. The two assasins jabbed Sun Ce with their spears.

We're Xu Gong's subordinates, here to avenge our master.

Kill them!

At this critical moment, Cheng Pu arrived with some men.

Cheng Pu and his men killed the assasins.

150

Sun Ce returned to the city but because the arrow was poisonous, his condition became critical.

Our country is in chaos. Please help my brother to achieve our goals!

Remember how our father established this territory. Guard it!

Mother, please take good care of younger brother.

Sun Ce handed his official seal to Sun Quan.

He's too young to shoulder the responsibility.

151

He's very talented. Consult Zhang Zhao and Zhou Yu on all matters.

Sun Ce died at the age of 26.

Zhou Yu attended Sun Ce's funeral, weeping bitterly.

I'll do my best.

How do I preserve the family's legacy?

Sun Quan asked Zhou Yu for advice.

152

You need capable and talented men.

Zhou Yu recommended Lu Su to assist Sun Quan.

Lu Su was well-educated and talented. He had foresight and great knowledge.

What should I do?

Suppress Huang Zu and attack Liu Biao. Then establish a kingdom east of the Changjiang.

Good, we'll do that.

Lu Su introduced Zhuge Jin to Sun Quan who appointed him as an advisor.

Cao Cao sent Zhang Hong back to Jiangdong and appointed Sun Quan as general and the Governor of Kuaiji.

Hence, Sun Quan established his reputation and won the people's support. The Jiangdong base was to become one of the three kingdoms.

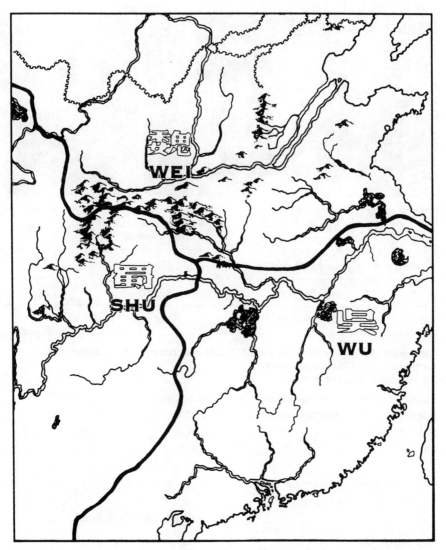

Appendix: Map of China during the Three Kingdoms Period

CLASSICS IN COMICS

Title	Price S$ (GST incl., free postage)	Qty	Total
Romance of the Three Kingdoms (Vol. 1-10)	$58.50		
Water Margin (Vol. 1-6)	$35.10		
水浒传 (第一至第六集)	$36.80		

Nett prices indicated after discount (GST incl.). Free postage for Singapore only.
Surface mail: S$5.00 for every book.
Air mail: S$8.00 for every book.

I wish to purchase the above-mentioned titles at the nett price of S$ _____

Enclosed is my postal order/money order/cheque for S$_____ (No.: _____)

Name (Mr/Mrs/Ms) _____ Tel _____

Address _____

_____ Fax _____

Please charge the amount of S$ _____ to my VISA/MASTER CARD account

(only Visa/Master Card accepted)

Card No. _____ Card Expiry Date _____

Card Holder's Name _____ Signature _____

Send to:

ASIAPAC BOOKS PTE LTD
996 Bendemeer Road #06-09 Singapore 339944 Tel: (65)63928455 Fax: (65)63926455
E-mail: asiapacbooks@pacific.net.sg   Website: www.asiapacbooks.com
Note: Prices include GST and are valid for purchase by mail order only. Prices subject to change without prior notice.

CHINESE CULTURE SERIES

Capture the essence of Chinese culture in comics

Title	*Price S$	Qty	Total
Origins of Chinese Festivals	$14.30		
Origins of Chinese Cuisine	$14.30		
Origins of Chinese People and Customs	$7.70		
Origins of Chinese Music and Art	$7.70		
Origins of Chinese Folk Arts	$7.70		
Origins of Chinese Martial Arts (Jun 2002)	$7.70		
Origins of Chinese Food and Drinks (Sep 2002)	$7.70		
Origins of Chinese Medicine (Dec 2002)	$7.70		

* Nett prices indicated after discount (GST incl.). Free postage for Singapore only.
Note: For overseas orders, please include postage fees:
Surface mail: S$5.00 for every book.
Air mail: S$8.00 for every book.

I wish to purchase the above-mentioned titles at the nett price of S$ _____

Enclosed is my postal order/money order/cheque for S$_____ (No.: _____)

Name (Mr/Mrs/Ms) _____ Tel _____

Address_____

_____ Fax _____

Please charge the amount of S$ _____ to my VISA/MASTER CARD account

(only Visa/Master Card accepted)

Card No. _____ Card Expiry Date _____

Card Holder's Name _____ Signature _____

Send to:

ASIAPAC BOOKS PTE LTD
996 Bendemeer Road #06-09 Singapore 339944 Tel: (65)63928455 Fax: (65)63926455
E-mail: asiapacbooks@pacific.net.sg   Website: www.asiapacbooks.com
Note: Prices include GST and are valid for purchase by mail order only. Prices
subject to change without prior notice.

Asiapac Web Site

Visit us at our Internet home page for
more information on Asiapac titles.

Asiapac Books Homepage
www.asiapacbooks.com

You will find:
- Asiapac — The Company
- Asiapac Logo
- Asiapac Publications
- Comics Extracts
- Book Reviews
- New Publications
- Ordering Our Publications

Or drop us a line at:
sales@asiapacbooks.com *(for ordering books)*
asiapacbooks@pacific.net.sg *(for general correspondence)*

三国演义
（第二册）

原著 ： 罗贯中

改编 ： 张企荣

绘画 ： 李成立

翻译 ： 殷书训

亚太图书有限公司出版